How the Dragon was Tricked

and other silly stories

Compiled by Vic Parker

Miles
KeLLy

First published in 2013 by Miles Kelly Publishing Ltd
Harding's Barn, Bardfield End Green, Thaxted, Essex, CM6 3PX, UK

2 4 6 8 10 9 7 5 3 1

Publishing Director Belinda Gallagher
Creative Director Jo Cowan
Editorial Director Rosie McGuire
Senior Editor Carly Blake
Editorial Assistant Amy Johnson
Designer Joe Jones
Production Manager Elizabeth Collins
Reprographics Stephan Davis, Jennifer Hunt, Thom Allaway

ISBN 978-1-84810-926-1

Printed in China

British Library Cataloguing-in-Publication Data
A catalogue record for this book is available from the British Library

ACKNOWLEDGMENTS

The publishers would like to thank the following artists who have contributed to this book:

Beehive Illustration Agency: Rosie Brooks, Mike Phillips
The Bright Agency: Michael Garton (inc. cover)
Jan Lewis, Aimee Mappley (decorative frames)

All other artwork from the Miles Kelly Artwork Bank

Made with paper from a sustainable forest

www.mileskelly.net   info@mileskelly.net

www.factsforprojects.com

Contents

Buttercup

By Sir George Webbe Dasent

Once upon a time there was an old wife who sat and baked. Now, you must know that this old wife had a little son, who was so plump and fat and so fond of good things, that they called him Buttercup. She had a dog, too, whose name was Goldtooth. One day, as she was baking, all at once Goldtooth began to bark.

"Run out, Buttercup, there's a dear," said

the old wife, "and see what Goldtooth is barking at."

So the boy ran out, and came back crying out, "Oh, heaven help us! Here comes a great big, ugly, old witch with a bag on her back."

"Jump under the table and hide yourself," said his mother.

Then in came the old hag. "Good day," said she.

"God bless you!" said Buttercup's mother.

"Isn't your Buttercup at home today?" asked the hag.

"No, that he isn't. He's out in the wood with his father."

"Plague take it," said the hag, "for I had a little silver knife I wanted to give him."

"Pip, pip! Here I am," said Buttercup from under the table, and out he came.

"I'm so old and stiff in the back," said the hag, "you must creep into the bag and fetch it out for yourself."

So Buttercup opened the bag and crept inside it. But as soon as he was well inside, the hag threw the bag over her back and strode off.

When they had gone a good bit of the way, the old hag got tired and asked, "How far is it to Snoring?"

"Half a mile," answered Buttercup.

So the hag put the sack down on the road, and went by herself into the wood and lay down to sleep. Meanwhile, Buttercup set to work and cut a hole in the sack with his knife. Then he crept out and put the great root of a fir tree into the sack, and ran home to his mother. When the hag got home and discovered what was in the sack, she was in a fine rage.

Next day the old wife sat and baked again, and her dog began to bark, just as he did the day before. "Run out, Buttercup, my boy," said she, "and see what Goldtooth is barking at."

"Well, I never!" cried Buttercup as soon as he looked outside. "If it isn't that ugly old beast coming again with a great sack on her back."

"Under the table with you and hide," said his mother.

"Good day!" said the hag. "Is your Buttercup at home today?"

"I'm sorry to say he isn't," said his mother, "he's out in the wood with his father."

"What a bore!" said the hag, "here I have a beautiful little silver spoon I want to give him."

"Pip, pip! Here I am," said Buttercup, and he crept out.

"I'm so stiff in the back," said the old witch, "you must creep into the sack and fetch it out for yourself."

So when Buttercup was well into the sack, the hag swung it over her shoulders and set off home as fast as her legs could carry her. But when they had gone a good bit she grew tired, and asked, "How far is it to Snoring?"

"A mile and a half," answered Buttercup.

So the hag set down the sack, and went into the wood to sleep a bit. While she slept, Buttercup made a hole in the sack and got out, and put a great stone into it instead.

When the old witch got home she made a great fire and put a big pot on it, and got everything ready to boil up Buttercup. But when she took the sack and thought she was going to turn out Buttercup into the pot, down plumped the stone and made a hole in the bottom, so that the water ran out and quenched the fire. Then the old hag was in a dreadful rage, and said, "Even if he makes himself ever so heavy next time, he won't trick me again."

On the third day, everything went just as it had gone twice before. Goldtooth began to bark, and Buttercup's mother said to him, "Run and see what our dog is barking at."

So out he went, but he soon came back crying out, "Heaven save us! Here comes the old hag again with a sack on her back."

"Jump under the table quick and hide," said his mother.

"Good day!" said the old hag, as she came in at the door. "Is your Buttercup at home today?"

"You're very kind to ask after him," said his mother, "but Buttercup's out in the wood with his father."

"What a bore, now," said the old hag. "Here have I got such a beautiful little silver fork for him."

"Pip, pip! Here I am," said Buttercup, as he came out from his hiding place.

"I'm so stiff in the back," said the hag, "you must creep into the sack and fetch it out for yourself."

But when Buttercup was well inside the sack the old hag swung it across her shoulders, and set off as fast as she could. This time she did not stop to sleep on the way, but went straight home with Buttercup in the sack.

It was Sunday, so the old hag said to her daughter, "Now you must take Buttercup and cook him up nicely till I come back, for I'm off to church to ask my guests to come for dinner."

So, when all in the house had gone to church, the daughter was to kill Buttercup, but she didn't know how to set about it.

"Stop a bit," said Buttercup, "I'll show you how to do it. Just lay your head on the chopping block, and you'll soon see."

So the poor silly thing laid her head down, and Buttercup took an ax and chopped off her head, just as if she had been a chicken.

Then Buttercup took all the gold and silver that lay in the old hag's house, and went home to his mother, and became a rich man.

Wishing for Wings

An extract from *Five Children and It*
by E Nesbit

Five children – Cyril, Anthea, Robert, Jane and the youngest, a baby whom they call 'the Lamb' – move house from London to the countryside in Kent, England. In a gravel pit near their home, they discover a strange creature called a Psammead, or Sand-fairy. He is able to grant one wish per day, and, over the next three days, he grants the children their wishes to become beautiful, to have heaps of gold coins and for the Psammead to be wanted by everyone. Each foolish wish causes the children to run into trouble. Fortunately, every day the Psammead's magic lasts only till sunset…

Have you ever been up at five o'clock on a fine summer morning? It is very beautiful. The sunlight is pinky and yellowy, and all

the grass and trees are covered with dew-
diamonds. All the shadows go the opposite
way to the way they do in the evening,
which is very interesting and makes you feel
as though you were in a new other world.

Anthea awoke at five. She had made
herself wake, and I must tell you how it is
done, even if it keeps you waiting for the
story to go on.

You get into bed at night, and lie down
quite flat on your little back with your
hands straight down by your sides. Then
you say "I must wake up at five" (or six, or
seven, or eight, or nine, or whatever the time
is that you want), and as you say it you
push your chin down on to your chest and
then bang your head back on the pillow.

And you do this as many times as there are ones in the time you want to wake up at. (It is quite an easy sum.) Of course everything depends on your really wanting to get up at five (or six, or seven, or eight, or nine). If you don't really want to, it's all of no use. But if you do – well, try it and see. Of course in this, as in doing Latin prose or getting into mischief, practise makes perfect. Anthea was quite perfect.

At the very moment when she opened her eyes, Anthea heard the black-and-gold clock down in the dining room strike eleven. So she knew it was three minutes to five. The black-and-gold clock always struck wrong, but it was all right when you knew what it meant. It was like a person

talking a foreign language. If you know the
language it is just as easy to understand as
English. And Anthea knew the clock
language.

She was very sleepy, but she jumped out
of bed and put her face and hands into a
basin of cold water. This
is a fairy charm
that prevents your
wanting to get
back into bed
again. Then she
dressed, and
folded up her
nightgown. She
did not tumble
it together by

17

the sleeves, but instead folded it by the
seams from the hem, and that will show
you the kind of well brought-up little girl
she was.

Then Anthea took her shoes in her hand
and crept softly down the stairs. She opened
the dining room window and climbed out.
It would have been just as easy to go out by
the door, but the window was more
romantic, and less likely to be noticed by
Martha, the nanny.

"I will always get up at five," Anthea said
to herself. "It is quite too awfully pretty for
anything."

Her heart was beating very fast, for she
was carrying out a plan quite her own. She
could not be sure that it was a good plan,

but she was quite sure that it would not be any better if she were to tell the others about it. And she had a feeling that, right or wrong, she would rather go through with it alone.

Anthea put on her shoes under the iron balcony, on the red and yellow shining tiles. Then she ran straight to the sandpit. She quickly found the Psammead's place and dug it out.

It was very cross indeed.

"It's too bad," it said, fluffing up its fur like pigeons do their feathers at Christmas time. "The weather's arctic, and it's the middle of the night."

"I'm so sorry," said Anthea gently. She took off her white apron and covered the

Sand-fairy up with it, all but its head, its bat's ears, and its eyes that were like a snail's eyes.

"Thank you," it said, "that's better. What's the wish this morning?"

"I don't know," said she, "that's just it. You see, we've been very unlucky so far. I wanted to talk to you about it. But – would you mind not giving me any wishes till after breakfast? It's so hard to talk to anyone if they jump out at you with wishes you don't really want!"

"You shouldn't say you wish for things if you don't wish for them."

"I'll try not to," said Anthea, "but I do wish—"

"Look out!" said the Psammead in a

warning voice, and it began to blow itself out.

"Oh, this isn't a magic wish — it's just — I should be so glad if you'd not swell yourself out and nearly burst to give me anything just now. Wait till the others are here."

"Well, well," it said indulgently, but it shivered.

"Would you like to come and sit on my lap?" asked Anthea kindly. "You'd be warmer, and I could turn the skirt of my frock up round you. I'd be very careful."

Anthea had never expected that it would, but it did.

"Thank you," it said, "you really are rather thoughtful." It crept on to her lap and snuggled down, and she put her arms

21

round it with a rather frightened gentleness.

"Well then," said Anthea, "everything we have wished has turned out rather horrid. I wish you would advise us. You are so old, you must be very wise."

"I was always generous from a child," said the Sand-fairy. "I've spent the whole of my waking hours giving. But one thing I won't give – that's advice."

"You see," Anthea went on, "it's such a wonderful thing. It's so good and kind of you to give us our wishes, and it seems such a pity it should all be wasted just because we are too silly to know what to wish for."

"Child," said the Sand-fairy sleepily, "I can only advise you to think before you speak…"

"But I thought you never gave advice."

"That piece doesn't count," it said. "You'll never take it! Besides, it's not original. It's in all the textbooks."

"But won't you just say if you think wings would be a silly wish?"

"Wings?" it said. "I should think you might do worse. Only, take care you aren't flying high at sunset. There was a little Ninevite boy I heard of once. He was one of King Sennacherib's sons, and a traveler

23

brought him a Psammead. He used to keep it in a box of sand on the palace terrace.

"One day," continued the Sand-fairy, "he wished for wings and got them. But at sunset, the wings turned into stone, and he fell slap onto one of the winged lions at the top of his father's great staircase. But I believe the boy enjoyed himself very much till then… Goodbye. I *am* so sleepy."

It jumped off her lap, dug frantically, and vanished.

Anthea was late for breakfast. Afterward, she and the others went back to the sand-pit, without the Lamb. In the lane Anthea, breathless from scurrying about, panted out, "I want to propose we take turns to wish. Only, nobody's to have a wish if the others don't think it's a nice wish. Do you agree?"

"Who's to have first wish?" asked Robert.

"Me, if you don't mind," said Anthea apologetically. "And I've thought about it – and it's wings."

"Not so dusty," said Cyril generously, and Robert added, "Really, Panther, you're not quite such a fool as you look."

Jane said, "I think it would be perfectly lovely. It's like a bright, joyful dream."

They found the Sand-fairy easily.

Anthea said, "I wish we all had beautiful wings to fly with."

The Sand-fairy blew himself out, and then each child felt a feeling, half heaviness and half lightness, on its shoulders.

Then the Psammead turned its snail's eyes from one child to the other. "Not so dusty," it said. "But really, Robert, you're not quite such an angel as you look." Robert almost blushed.

The wings were very big, and more beautiful than you can possibly imagine – for they were soft and smooth, and every feather lay neatly in its place. And the feathers were of the most lovely mixed changing colors, like a rainbow, or iridescent glass, or the beautiful scum that sometimes floats on water.

"Oh – but can we fly?" Jane said, standing anxiously, first on one foot and then on the other.

"Look out!" said Cyril. "You're treading on my wing."

"Does it hurt?" asked Anthea, but no one answered, for Robert had spread his wings and jumped up, and now he was rising in the air. And then they all spread their wings and followed him into the skies.

Their wings were tremendously wide

27

when they were spread out, and they had to fly quite a long way apart so as not to get in each other's way.

All the words in the English Dictionary, and in the Greek Lexicon as well, are, I find, of no use at all to tell you what it feels like to be flying. But I will say that to look down on the fields and woods is like looking at a beautiful live map, where you have real moving sunny woods and green fields laid out one after the other. As Cyril said, and I can't think where he got such a strange expression, "It does you a fair treat!"

It was most wonderful and more like real magic than any wish the children had had yet…

The Lad and the Devil

By Sir George Webbe Dasent

Once upon a time there was a lad who was walking along a road cracking nuts. He found one that was worm-eaten, and just at that very moment he met the Devil.

"Is it true, now," said the lad, "what they say, that the Devil can make himself as small as he chooses, and thrust himself in through a pinhole?"

"Yes, it is," said the Devil.

"Oh! It is, is it? Then let me see you do it, and just creep into this nut," said the lad.

So the Devil did it.

Now, when he had crept well into the nut through the worm's hole, the lad stopped it up with a pin. "Now, I've got you safe," he said, and put the nut in his pocket.

When he had walked on a bit, he came to a smithy. He turned in and asked the smith if he'd be good enough to crack that nut for him.

"Ay, that'll be an easy job," said the smith. He took his smallest hammer, laid the nut on the anvil and gave it a blow, but it wouldn't break.

So he took another hammer a little bigger, but that wasn't heavy enough either.

Then he took one bigger still, but it was still the same story, and so the smith got angry, and grasped his great sledgehammer.

"Now, I'll crack you to bits," he said, and let drive at the nut with all his might and main. And so the nut flew to pieces with a bang that blew off half the roof of the smithy, and the whole house creaked and groaned as

31

though it were ready to fall.

"Why! The very Devil himself must have been in that nut," said the smith.

"So he was, you're quite right," said the lad, as he went away laughing.

How the Dragon was Tricked

By Andrew Lang

Once upon a time there lived a man who had two sons, but the elder son hated the younger son. One day, as they were walking through a wood, the elder youth seized hold of the other, tied him to a tree, and went on his way hoping that his brother might starve to death.

However, it happened that an old and humpbacked shepherd passed by and said,

"Tell me, my son, why are you tied to that tree?"

"Because I was so crooked," answered the young man, "but it has quite cured me, and now my back is as straight as can be."

"I wish you would bind me to a tree," exclaimed the shepherd, "so that my back would get straight."

"With pleasure," replied the youth. "If you will loosen these cords I will tie you up as firmly as I can."

This was soon done, and then the young man drove off with the shepherd's sheep.

By these and many other tricks the young man soon became so famous that the King demanded to see him. Soldiers captured him and brought him before the

King, who said, "Because of your tricks and pranks, you should, in the eye of the law, be put to death. But if you can bring me the flying horse that belongs to the great dragon, I will spare you."

When night came the young man made his way straight to the dragon's home and the flying horse's stable. He was stretching his hand cautiously out to seize the bridle, when the horse suddenly began to neigh as loud as he could. This woke the sleeping dragon, who was very angry to be disturbed and came to give the horse a beating. The horse was very upset, and when the dragon returned back to bed, he let the young man lead him quietly away.

The King said, "The flying horse is all

very well, but I want something more. You must bring me the covering with the little bells that lies on the bed of the dragon, or I will have you put to death."

When night came the young man went away to the dragon's house and climbed up onto the roof. Then he opened a little window in the roof and let down a rope and tried to hook the bed covering to draw it up. But the little bells began to ring, and the dragon woke and drew the covering toward him, pulling the young man into the room as he did so. Then the dragon flung himself on the youth and bound him fast. He roared to his wife, saying, "Tomorrow when I go out you must stay at home and kill him and cook him. When I get back

we will eat him together."

So the following morning the dragoness took hold of the young man, and reached up on the shelf for a sharp knife with which to kill him. But as she untied the cords the better to get hold of him, the prisoner seized her and threw her into the oven. Then he snatched up the bed covering and carried it to the King.

"That is not enough," said His Majesty. "Bring me the dragon himself, or I will have you put to death."

"It shall be done," answered the youth, and he disguised himself as a beggar and set out on the road to the dragon's house. The young man found his enemy in front of his house, very busy making a box. "What is the box for?" inquired the beggar.

"It is for the man who killed my wife, and stole my flying horse and my bed covering," said the dragon.

"He deserves nothing better," answered the beggar. "Still that box doesn't look big enough for a man."

"You are wrong," said the dragon. "The box is large enough even for me."

"Well, of course, if you can get in, he should be able to," the man said. "But I am sure you would find it a tight fit."

"No, there is plenty of room," said the dragon, tucking himself carefully inside.

But no sooner was he well in, than the
young man clapped the lid on tight, and
drove in nails to make it tighter still. Then
he took the box on his back and brought it
to the King. When the King heard that the
dragon was inside, he was so excited that he
would not wait. He broke the lock and
lifted the lid just a little way. The King was
very careful not to leave enough space for
the dragon to jump out, but unluckily there
was just room for his great mouth.

With one snap the very foolish King
vanished down his wide jaws. The young
man married the King's daughter and ruled
over the land, but what he did with the
dragon nobody knows.